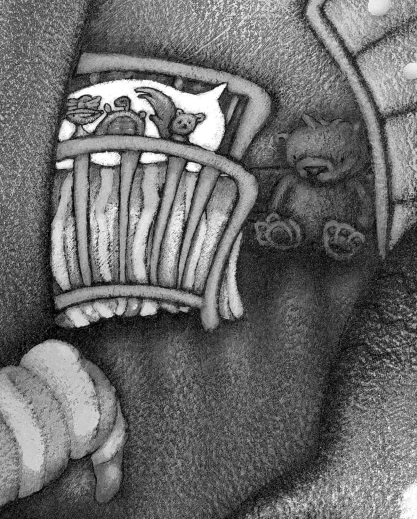

To all children
To my children
—*Ned Dickens*

For Jenn,
my foundation, my foil,
my friend, all of my love,
now and forever.
—*Graham Ross*

National Library of Canada Cataloguing in Publication Data:

Dickens, Ned

By a thread / story by Ned Dickens ; illustrations by Graham Ross.

ISBN 1-55143-325-7

I. Ross, Graham, 1962- II. Title.

PS8557.I256B9 2005   jC813'.54   C2004-906802-4

First published in the United States 2005

Library of Congress Control Number: 2004116126

Summary: In this rhyming story, when the toy box in Beo's bedroom erupts,
Beo and the toys must find a way back to safety.

Orca Book Publishers gratefully acknowledges the support for its publishing programs
provided by the following agencies: the Government of Canada through the Book Publishing Industry
Development Program (BPIDP), the Canada Council for the Arts, and the British Columbia Arts Council.

Art Director and design: Lynn O'Rourke
Printed and bound in Hong Kong

Orca Book Publishers
Box 5626 Stn. B
Victoria, BC Canada
V8R 6S4

Orca Book Publishers
PO Box 468
Custer, WA   USA
98240-0468

07 06 05 04 · 4 3 2 1

BY A THREAD

Story by
Ned Dickens

Illustrations by
Graham Ross

Orca Book Publishers

Beo, her buddies (old **Bard** and the others,
Like Curtis the tortoise and Ms. Alice Mouse)
Were busy pretending

And sure Beo's mother
was far away mending or writing
Or something, like fixing the house.

She couldn't have heard the magnificent

BOOM

 When the **toy box** volcano demolished the room.

BUT
SHE DID.

And she *sighed,*
and she climbed up the stairs

While the toys tried to hide

And she opened the door
and she *sighed,*

And she *sighed.*

Then she said (her thoughts deep in her head)

"*Where's the floor?*"

Only that,

"*Where's the floor?*"

Then she turned
and she left
and she said nothing more.

And they froze, and the hair on the hairier animals

r^oe on the back of their scalps,

And before you could say,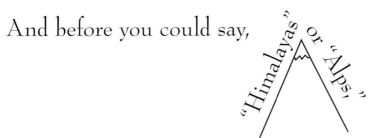

The floor (or the place where the floor was before)

Was an echoing **dizzying**

drop

so deep and so steep

From the bottomless bottom right up

to the top of the tippytoe top

That if something (or somebody!) fell,

you never would tell if it landed

Or just kept on falling

It was **really** that deep.
They were **really** that high.

Now **Bard**, the old bear, as is often the case,
Found himself in a cozy and comfortable place,
But the rest of the gang and Beo herself
Were hanging or clinging or clutching or swinging
On the edge of a ledge or a slippery shelf.

Old Sydney had made his way over the bookcase
And onto the shade of a lamp on the wall
(But he was afraid that the lampshade would fall).

And Alice the mouse was deeply uncertain
Exactly how long she could swing from the curtain.

And Curtis (poor Curtis!)
Had a slippery grip on the very thin,
Slowly unraveling thread, to which he had clung,
And by which he now hung,
From the blanket which,
less and less, covered the bed.

And Beo (let's whisper
so's not to distress her)
Had a teetery toehold
        on top of the dresser.

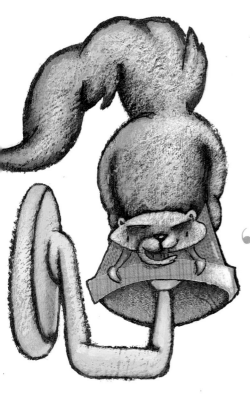

They were all,

"Except Bard,"

In a terrible fix

When **Bard** stood, cleared his throat, and said,

"**Beo**, your tricks of pretending
                 have done it again."

And then!

Just as he started to speak a great speech,
His perch gave a creak, then a lurch to the right,
He reached out his paw . . .

                              and he
                                   vanished from sight.

"Oh my goodness!"

"Excuse me. I think I'm all right.

I was on my way down to the bottomless floor,

But it seems I've been saved by

the underwear drawer."

"Now that's a relief."

So, in brief, each of the gang,

"Except Bard,"

Was hanging or trapped in a difficult place.

"Excuse me," sniffed Bard. "I'm allergic to lace."

"I sympathize, Bard," murmured Curtis politely,
"But, frankly, I think that you've landed quite lightly,
While I am, I think, at the end of my thread.
If I am and I fall, I'm afraid I'll be—"

"Wait!" shouted Alice.
"Before it's too late, cut all the commotion.
I've noticed a notion beginning to spin
in the back of my head!
We'll get out of this scrape!
I'll chew on the drape . . .
There, a thread. If I get it to Syd"
(And she did) "Then I bet we can get it to Curtis."

"And yet," said old Sydney, pulling it in,
"I'm afraid it's too thin to take all his weight.
It would break."

"It's really been wonderful

knowing you all, **But** my string has run out and I'm going to——",

"STOP!

Don't you give up!
You're not going to drop!
Tie together those tights."

"There's still hope!"

"Like this?
In a rope?"

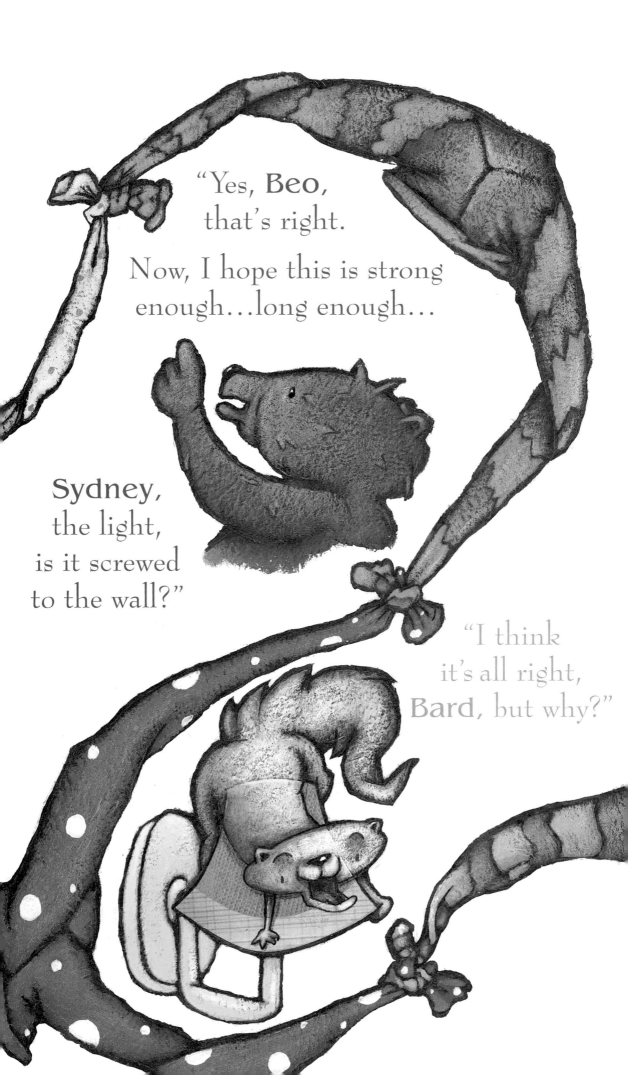

"Yes, **Beo**,
that's right.
Now, I hope this is strong
enough...long enough...

Sydney,
the light,
is it screwed
to the wall?"

"I think
it's all right,
Bard, but why?"

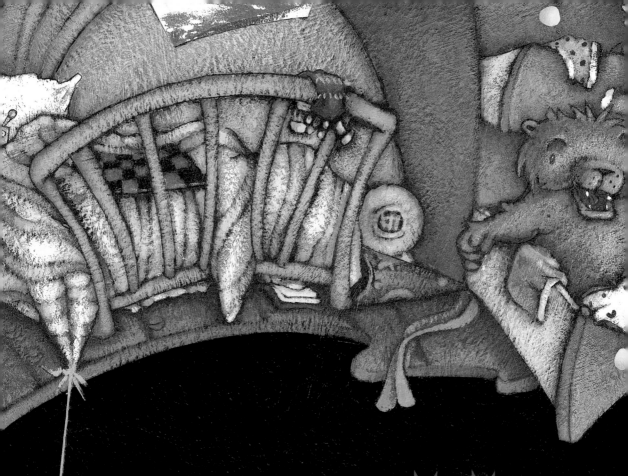

"Tie the thread to your hat now, **Ms. Mouse**.
Can you toss it across so that **Beo** can catch it?
Like that! Oh. Well done!"

"This is

"Now **Beo** attach it—"

"**To the end of the tights-ropy thing.**"

"Now **Sydney,** you bring it up high and tie it
as well as you can to the light on the wall

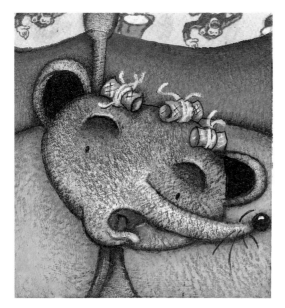

"Don't fall!!"

"I'm sinking."

"Please Curtis,

hang in there, be brave."

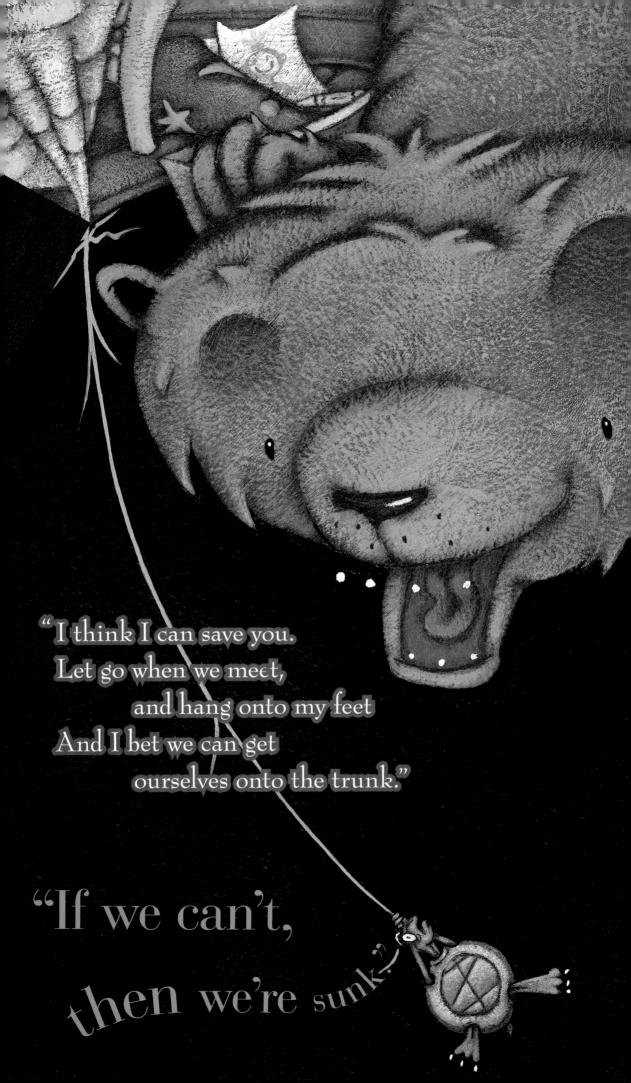

"I think I can save you.
Let go when we meet,
    and hang onto my feet
And I bet we can get
    ourselves onto the trunk."

"If we can't,
then we're sunk."

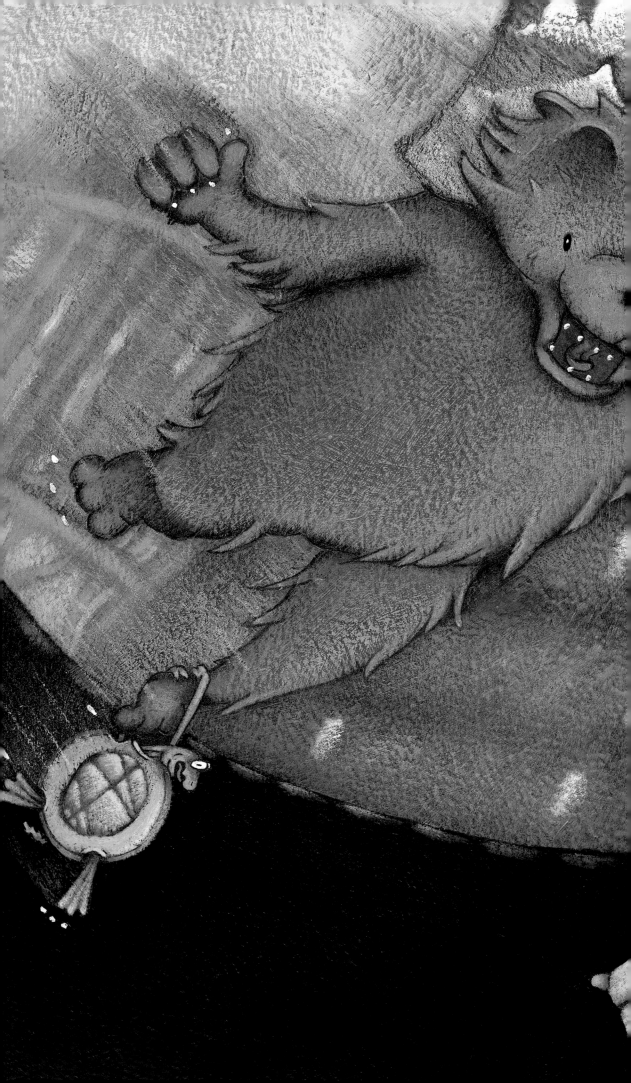

"Keep your eyes upon me,

One
two
three
and

YIPPEEE!!!"

With his tummy tucked in and a grim sort of grin
On his fuzzy old face, he dived into space.
And he streaked in a curve through the air,
And he gathered up Curtis, who hung on like mad
With the last little bit of hanging he had.
And they swung in a sweep,
And they landed together

KERPLUNK!

In a heap on the trunk!

"HOORAY!"

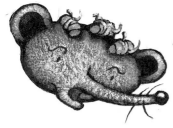

"I don't mean to fuss,
but what about us?"

"If you don't lose your heads,
you can get to the bed.
Now, give a big jump
and land on your rump."

That's your plan?"

"Well, if I can be brave,
friends, then anyone can!
You'll go first, won't you, **Syd**?"

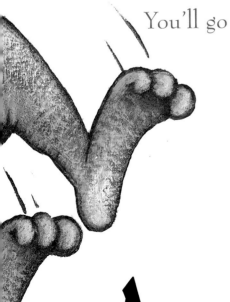

And he did!

"I propose we pretend
that this game's at an end,
And the floor is restored
just the same as before."

And before you could say,

"Give that Bear a big hug,"

They were leaping
and dancing around on the rug.

"Tell me, Bard, you old softy,
when did you get so lofty

"And clever?"

"And handsome?"

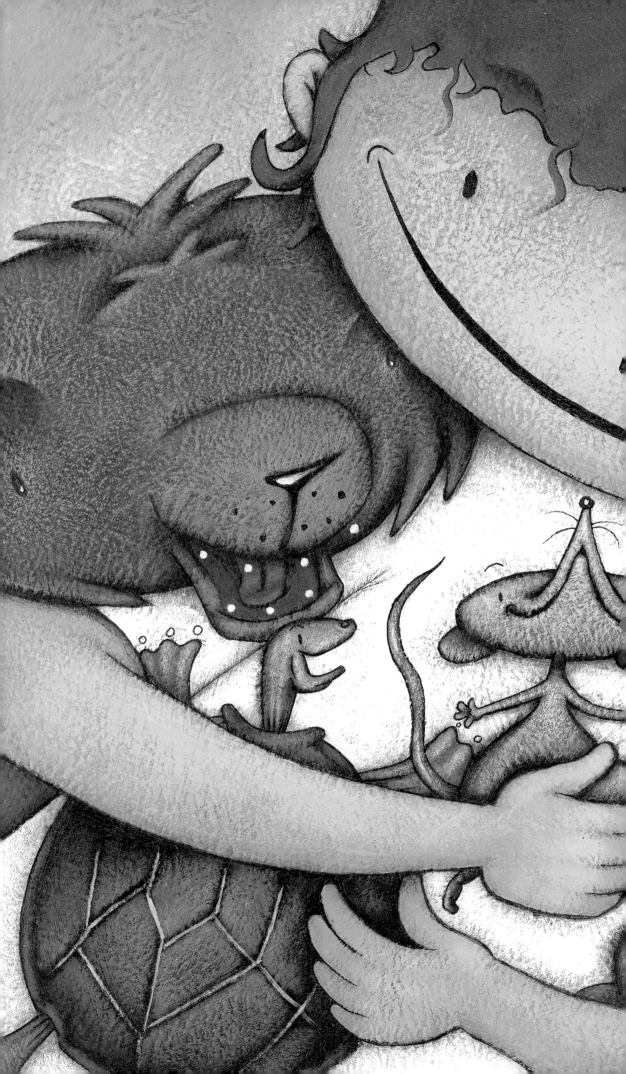

So, a muddle of
cuddles and then
the whole bunch
Headed out on
the perilous
journey to ...